THIS CANDLEWICK BOOK BELONGS TO:

_____

_____

_____

To Robyn, Susan, Meredith, Cyndy, Katie, Kim,
Mary Lou, and April, friends for the journey
D. H. A.

To choopmonkey, Anne-Marie
K. M.

Loony
Little

An Environmental Tale

Dianna Hutts Aston

illustrated by Kelly Murphy

CANDLEWICK PRESS
CAMBRIDGE, MASSACHUSETTS

On a cold summer night, when the Arctic sun was shining brightly, a drop of water fell — *plop!* — on Loony Little's head.

"Great top of the world!" she wailed. "The polar icecap is melting! I must go tell the Polar Bear Queen!"

Loony Little flew northward as fast as she could. On a high cliff she met Dovekie Lovekie.

"Where are you going, Loony Little?" asked Dovekie Lovekie.

"The polar icecap is melting, and I am going to tell the Polar Bear Queen," replied Loony Little.

"Goodness glaciers!" squawked Dovekie Lovekie. "Why is the icecap melting? I will come with you and ask the Polar Bear Queen."

The two flew northward as fast as they could until they spied Puffin Muffin floating on the sea.

"Where are you going?" asked Puffin Muffin.

"The polar icecap is melting, and we are going to tell the Polar Bear Queen," replied Loony Little and Dovekie Lovekie.

"Suffering puffalumps!" screeched Puffin Muffin. "If the icecap is melting, will the sea rise? I will come with you and ask the Polar Bear Queen."

The three swam along until they met Harey Clarey on the shore.

"Where are you going?" asked Harey Clarey.

"The polar icecap is melting, and we are going to tell the Polar Bear Queen," replied Loony Little, Dovekie Lovekie, and Puffin Muffin.

"Leaping lemmings!" snuffled Harey Clarey. "If the icecap is melting, will my den be flooded? I will come with you and ask the Polar Bear Queen."

So they all scooted and waddled and hopped northward until they met Sealy Sally coming up for a breath of air.

"Where are you going?" asked Sealy Sally.

"The polar icecap is melting, and we are going to tell the Polar Bear Queen," replied Loony Little, Dovekie Lovekie, Puffin Muffin, and Harey Clarey.

"Be careful!" barked Sealy Sally. "The Polar Bear Queen
ate my cousin just last week — she will eat all of you, too!"
Sealy Sally slipped back into the sea.

"Oh dear!" wailed Loony Little.

"Oh my!" squawked Dovekie Lovekie.

"Oh no!" screeched Puffin Muffin.

"Let's *not* tell the Polar Bear Queen!" snuffled Harey Clarey.

Just then Foxy Loxy appeared. "Where are you going in such a rush?" he asked.

"We *were* going to see the Polar Bear Queen," said Loony Little.

"To tell her the icecap is melting," said Dovekie Lovekie.

"But Sealy Sally told us the Polar Bear Queen is dangerous," said Puffin Muffin.

"So we are turning back," said Harey Clarey.

"Oh no, *please* don't turn back," said Foxy Loxy. "Not without delivering such *important* news."

"But the Polar Bear Queen might eat us!" wailed Loony Little.

"No, she won't," said Foxy Loxy. "Not if I escort you. Come, I will take you to her."

And so Loony Little, Dovekie Lovekie, Puffin Muffin, and Harey Clarey followed Foxy Loxy. But Loony Little, who couldn't waddle or hop as well as the others, fell behind.

"Wait for me!" cried Loony Little, tripping over something in the snow.

"Stop!" Loony Little wailed. "We've been tricked! That's Foxy Loxy's lair — he's going to eat us!"

Thinking quickly, she pecked a nugget of ice from the ground and flung it at Foxy Loxy. It hit him squarely on the head.

"Great midnight sun!" howled Foxy Loxy. "The polar icecap *is* melting!
I must go tell the Polar Bear Queen!"

In a blur of fur, he was gone.

Foxy Loxy found the Polar Bear Queen sprawled flat near a hole in the ice, waiting for Sealy Sally to come up for air.

"Quick, run for your life!" shouted Foxy Loxy.
"The polar icecap is melting!"

"How awful," roared the Polar Bear Queen.
"Tell me more — after dinner!"

And she ate Foxy Loxy.

Soon, the four friends were safe on a southerly course.

"Wow, the Polar Bear Queen *is* dangerous!" said Harey Clarey.

"And she doesn't seem to care about the icecap melting,"
said Puffin Muffin.

"I guess we'll have to find someone who *will* care,"
said Dovekie Lovekie.

"Like who?" asked Loony Little.

AUTHOR'S NOTE

Today, scientists are studying conditions in the Arctic, trying to find out whether changes in the polar icecap are natural or are the result of global warming caused by humans.

Here's what they have discovered:

- **In recent years, the Arctic Ocean's polar icecap has become smaller and thinner.**

- **Glaciers are also becoming smaller.**

- **Warmer Atlantic Ocean waters have pushed into the Arctic Ocean, causing Arctic sea temperatures to rise by about two degrees Fahrenheit.**

- **The average surface temperature of the earth has risen by one degree Fahrenheit in the last one hundred years.**

What will happen if the polar icecap melts? No one knows for sure. Some scientists say climate and weather all over the world would change, causing floods, blizzards, and droughts.

Other scientists say there is no cause for alarm because our pollution is not significant enough to cause drastic changes in the earth's weather.

One thing is certain: We must continue to study and understand the changing conditions in the Arctic so that we can protect the creatures that call it home.

For more information, visit the following websites:

National Snow and Ice Data Center
http://nsidc.org

Polar Science Center
http://psc.apl.washington.edu

ABOUT THE ANIMALS

COMMON LOON   The common loon has a call that can sound like a wail, a laugh, or even a yodel. The loon is a skilled swimmer, diver, and flier — however, because its webbed feet are close to its tail, it waddles on land by pushing itself along on its chest.

DOVEKIE   These small birds are a favorite prey of Arctic foxes. During the summer, when the sun shines even at midnight, millions of dovekies swarm toward their nesting grounds, forming fluttering black ribbons that can stretch for miles over the waves.

ATLANTIC PUFFIN   A short-necked bird that spends most of its time on the sea, the puffin returns to land only to nest. Its beak becomes bright orange and yellow during mating season. Some puffins live to be forty years old.

ARCTIC HARE Arctic hares of the Far North keep their white coats year-round and travel in large herds. Their wide hind paws act as snowshoes so that hares can move quickly across the snow. The Arctic hare can hop away on two legs, as a kangaroo does.

SEAL The seal can hold its breath underwater for twenty minutes or more. When the seas freeze over in winter, seals make breathing holes in the ice. Polar bears often catch seals at or near the surface of their breathing holes.

ARCTIC FOX An adult Arctic fox weighs about as much as a house cat, but its bushy coat— white in winter, brownish gray in summer — makes it look much larger. Foxes follow polar bears and feed on their leftovers. They also eat small mammals, birds, and bird eggs.

POLAR BEAR The largest, most powerful hunter in the Arctic, the polar bear wanders the polar ice, hunting seal, its favorite food. With its webbed front paws, the polar bear is also an excellent swimmer and can swim a distance of sixty miles in search of food.

First paperback edition 2007

The Library of Congress has cataloged the hardcover edition as follows:
Aston, Dianna Hutts.
Loony Little / Dianna Hutts Aston ; illustrated by Kelly Murphy. —1st ed.
p.   cm.
Summary: In a plot similar to the traditional tale of Chicken Little, Loony Little fears
that the polar icecap is melting and, along with other animals, travels to alert the Polar Bear Queen.
Includes notes on global warming and Arctic animals.
ISBN 978-0-7636-1682-3 (hardcover)
[1. Global warming—Fiction. 2. Loons—Fiction. 3. Animals—Fiction. 4. Polar regions—Fiction.]
I. Murphy, Kelly, ill. II. Title.
PZ7.A8483 Lo 2003
[E] — dc21   2002067696

ISBN 978-0-7636-3562-6 (paperback)

2 4 6 8 10 9 7 5 3 1

Printed in China

This book was typeset in Badger Light.
The illustrations were done in acrylic, watercolor, and gel medium on board.

Candlewick Press
2067 Massachusetts Avenue
Cambridge, Massachusetts 02140

visit us at www.candlewick.com

Dianna Hutts Aston is also the author of *When You Were Born*, illustrated by E. B. Lewis. About *Loony Little*, she says, "It was one of the hottest summer days on record. My mind, of its own accord, kept wandering northward, to a wilderness of snow and ice, the Artic. While listening to the news one evening, I heard Peter Jennings say, 'The polar icecap is melting—or is it?' The phrase 'The sky is falling!' came to me immediately. So the whole concept for *Loony Little* just fell into my mind." Dianna Hutts Aston lives in central Texas with her husband and two children.

Kelly Murphy lives in southeastern Massachusetts, where snow is a familiar friend. She is a graduate of the Rhode Island School of Design and is the illustrator of *Good Babies: A Tale of Trolls, Humans, a Witch, and a Switch* by Tim Myers.